SPOOkerMARKET

To Lucy, for the inspiration, as ever – P. B.

For VRM & SB, keeping it spooky all year long! – S. L.

PUFFIN BOOKS

UK | USA | Canada | Ireland | Australia | India | New Zealand | South Africa

Puffin Books is part of the Penguin Random House group of companies whose addresses can be found at global.penguinrandomhouse.com.

www.penguin.co.uk   www.puffin.co.uk   www.ladybird.co.uk

Penguin Random House UK

First published 2022

001

Printed and bound in China

The authorized representative in the EEA is Penguin Random House Ireland, Morrison Chambers, 32 Nassau Street, Dublin D02 YH68

A CIP catalogue record for this book is available from the British Library

ISBN: 978–0–241–47304–7

All correspondence to:
Puffin Books, Penguin Random House Children's, One Embassy Gardens, 8 Viaduct Gardens, London SW11 7BW

SPOOkerMARKET

PETER BENTLY & STEPH LABERIS

PUFFIN

Where do **werewolves** get their greens?

Where do
banshees buy
their beans?

Where do **ogres** get supplies
of tasty ear-and-eyeball pies?

THE... SPOOKerMARKET

That's the place!
Where **Queenie Sweeney's** smiling face
welcomes every ghoul and fright
who does their shopping in the night.

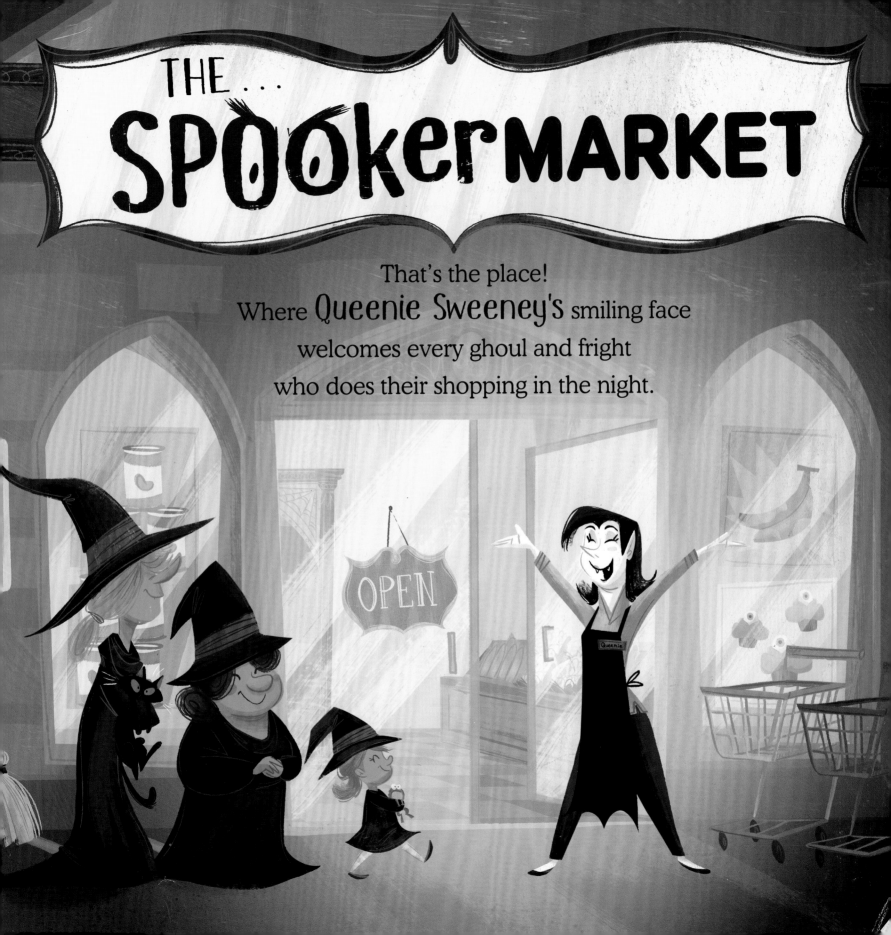

One evening, near the fruit and veg,
the vegan vampire, old **Sir Reg**,

48p

was chatting to a friendly group
of **witches** buying toad-leg soup . . .

when **Flaky Jakey** shuffled in,
trailing
flakes
of
greenish
skin.

"Those zombies!"
moaned the cleaner, Lurk.
"Always making extra work!"

Lurk brushed up the flakes of skin
and popped them in the nearest bin.
The bin was next to Till Thirteen.
Lurk sighed, "That checkout needs a clean!"

He grabbed his cloth and cleaning spray
to wipe the dust and dirt away.

But **Queenie Sweeney** cried out, "Wait!
That till is cursed! Oh no! Too late!"

Till Thirteen began to quake.

(A startled werewolf dropped her cake.)

The till flew open – "Yikes!" wailed Queenie.

"Lurk has woken up . . .

. . . the GENIE!"

"Yay!" the genie cried. "YIPPEE!
Shazzoo-Shazzam! At last I'm free!
Nice to meet you, everyone!
It's time to have some genie fun!

Abracadabra!
Abracadee!

First he snatched off Jakey's head
and put a pumpkin on instead.

(Jakey didn't seem to mind.
Zombies aren't that bright, I find.)

Then the genie grabbed some fruit.

"Let's go bowling!
What a hoot!"

Corn on the
Cobweb
78p

Along the floor the melons rumbled . . .
One by one the mummies tumbled.

The genie, with a naughty smile,
whizzed along the baking aisle,
in and out of people's legs,
bombarding them with flour and eggs.

He spotted two great trolls ahead
and pelted them with crusty bread.
"What's wrong?" The genie grinned with glee.
"It's freshly baked and gluten-free!"

Queenie cried, "I wish you'd stop!
You're going to trash my whole darned shop!"

The genie smirked. "I don't DO wishes!
How about some three-eyed fishes?

Or slime to soothe your scabs
and itches?

Or toasted toenails
– SO delicious!

And don't forget those
dirty dishes!"

Queenie wailed, "I need a plan!
Ah, there's Sir Reg. The very man!
"Quickly, Reg!" she said. "Come here!
I need to whisper in your ear!"

The genie zoomed around the store,
causing ballyhoo galore.
He met Sir Reg, who swished his cape
and said, "I bet you can't change shape!"

Reg went POP!
and, just like that,
became a flapping
vampire BAT.

"Call that clever? Don't be daft!
Just watch THIS!" The genie laughed.

"Abracadabra! Abracadee!

Who's the greatest genie?

ME!"

AISLE 5

Queenie said, "Not bad at all.
But I bet you can't go REALLY small."
The genie cackled. "SMALL, you say?
Easy-peasy! Right away!

Abracadabra!
Abracadee!
Who's the
greatest genie?
ME!

How about a snail?

A slug?

A spider? Or . . .

Queenie didn't stop and think.
She grabbed the insect in a blink.

Till Thirteen stood open wide.
Queenie popped the bug inside.
And before you could say

"Shazzoo-
shazzam!" . . .

She shut the cash drawer with a SLAM!
They heard the genie's furious shout:
"You rascals tricked me! Let me out!"

Lurk the cleaner said,

"No way! You've caused me
too much grief today!
Look at all this horrid mess!"

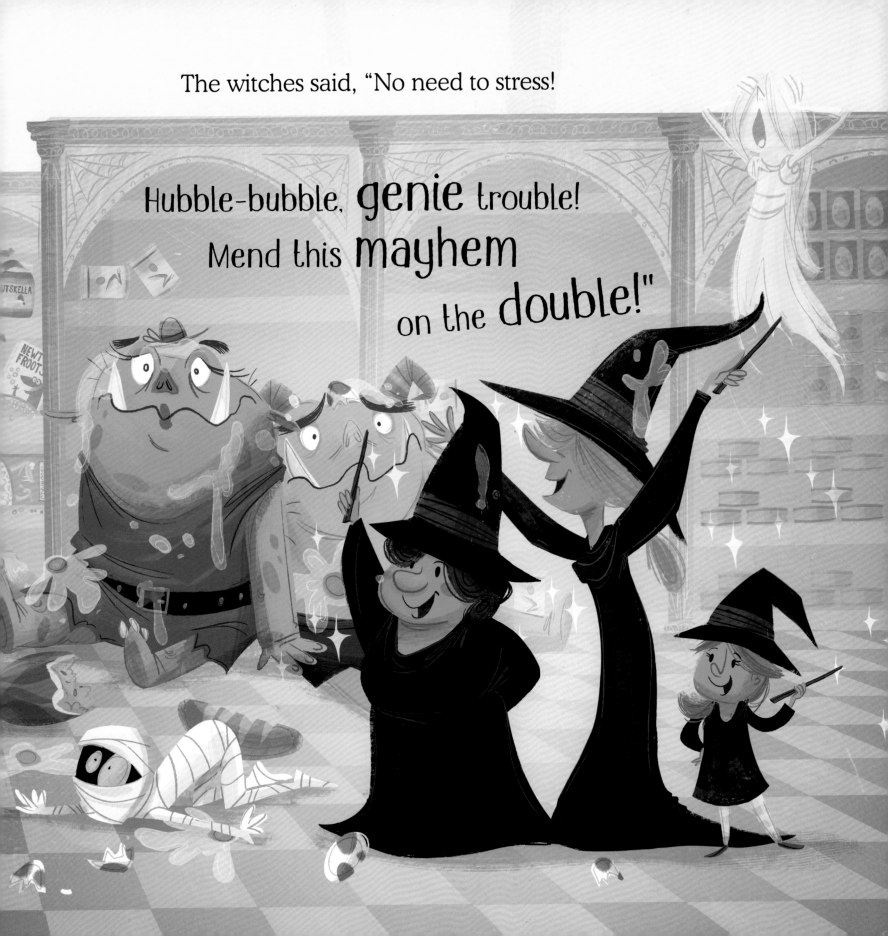

The witches said, "No need to stress!

Hubble-bubble, genie trouble!
Mend this mayhem
on the double!"

WHOOSH! A flash of magic light
set the SPOOKERMARKET right!
"One last thing," the witches said.

AISLE 5

BOONANAS 98P

And – WHOOSH! – they put back Jakey's head!

"Thanks!" smiled Queenie. "Now, let's eat!
No more tricks. Instead – a TREAT!"

"Help yourself to **cockroach cake!**
Or **eyeball pie!**
Or **slug-slime shake!**

The **Spookermarket** cafe's FREE!
Let's **celebrate!**
It's all on **me!**"

And that's why every ghost and fright
and other ghouls who roam the night –
like witches, werewolves and the rest –
say "Spookermarket is the BEST!"